LITTLE SEEDS

By NADIA HIGGINS

Illustrations by CHRIS BIGGIN

Music by DREW TEMPERANTE

CANTATA LEARNING

WWW.CANTATALEARNING.COM

CANTATA LEARNING

Published by Cantata Learning
1710 Roe Crest Drive
North Mankato, MN 56003
www.cantatalearning.com

Copyright © 2018 Cantata Learning

All rights reserved. No part of this publication may be reproduced in any form without written permission from the publisher.

A note to educators and librarians from the publisher: Cantata Learning has provided the following data to assist in book processing and suggested use of Cantata Learning product.

Publisher's Cataloging-in-Publication Data
Prepared by Librarian Consultant: Ann-Marie Begnaud
Library of Congress Control Number: 2016938075
  Little Seeds
  Series: My First Science Songs
  By Nadia Higgins
  Illustrations by Chris Biggin
  Music by Drew Temperante
  Summary: Learn how seeds help new plants grow in this illustrated story set to music.
  ISBN: 978-1-63290-787-5 (library binding/CD)
  ISBN: 978-1-68410-110-8 (paperback)
Suggested Dewey and Subject Headings:
  Dewey: E 575.68
  LCSH Subject Headings: Seeds – Juvenile literature. | Seeds – Songs and music – Texts. | Seeds – Juvenile sound recordings.
  Sears Subject Headings: Seeds. | School songbooks. | Children's songs. | Popular music.
  BISAC Subject Headings: JUVENILE NONFICTION / Science & Nature / Flowers & Plants. | JUVENILE NONFICTION / Music / Songbooks. | JUVENILE NONFICTION / Science & Nature / Botany.

Book design and art direction: Tim Palin Creative
Editorial direction: Flat Sole Studio
Music direction: Elizabeth Draper
Music written and produced by Drew Temperante

ACCESS THE MUSIC!
SCAN CODE WITH MOBILE APP
CANTATALEARNING.COM

Printed in the United States   4835

TIPS TO SUPPORT LITERACY AT HOME

WHY READING AND SINGING WITH YOUR CHILD IS SO IMPORTANT

Daily reading with your child leads to increased academic achievement. Music and songs, specifically rhyming songs, are a fun and easy way to build early literacy and language development. Music skills correlate significantly with both phonological awareness and reading development. Singing helps build vocabulary and speech development. And reading and appreciating music together is a wonderful way to strengthen your relationship.

READ AND SING EVERY DAY!

TIPS FOR USING CANTATA LEARNING BOOKS AND SONGS DURING YOUR DAILY STORY TIME

1. As you sing and read, point out the different words on the page that rhyme. Suggest other words that rhyme.

2. Memorize simple rhymes such as Itsy Bitsy Spider and sing them together. This encourages comprehension skills and early literacy skills.

3. Use the questions in the back of each book to guide your singing and storytelling.

4. Read the included sheet music with your child while you listen to the song. How do the music notes correlate to the words of the song?

5. Sing along on the go and at home. Access music by scanning the QR code on each Cantata book. You can also stream or download the music for free to your computer, smartphone, or mobile device.

Devoting time to daily reading shows that you are available for your child. Together, you are building language, literacy, and listening skills.

Have fun reading and singing!

Did you ever wonder where plants come from? They grow from little seeds. And where do little seeds come from? They grow on plants.

To learn more about little seeds, turn the page and sing along!

5

One, two, three, four, five, six!
Six plant parts and they go like this:
roots, stems, leaves,
flowers, fruit, and seeds!

fruit

seed

flower

leaf

stem

root

Each part plays a special role.
Seeds help plants grow and grow.

Little seeds hold big surprises
of new plants yet to come.

Give seeds warmth. Give them water.
A plant could grow from every one.

9

A seed has three parts to help it grow.
A baby plant—that's the **embryo**.

The rest is food to give it a start.
A tough seed **coat** forms the outside part.

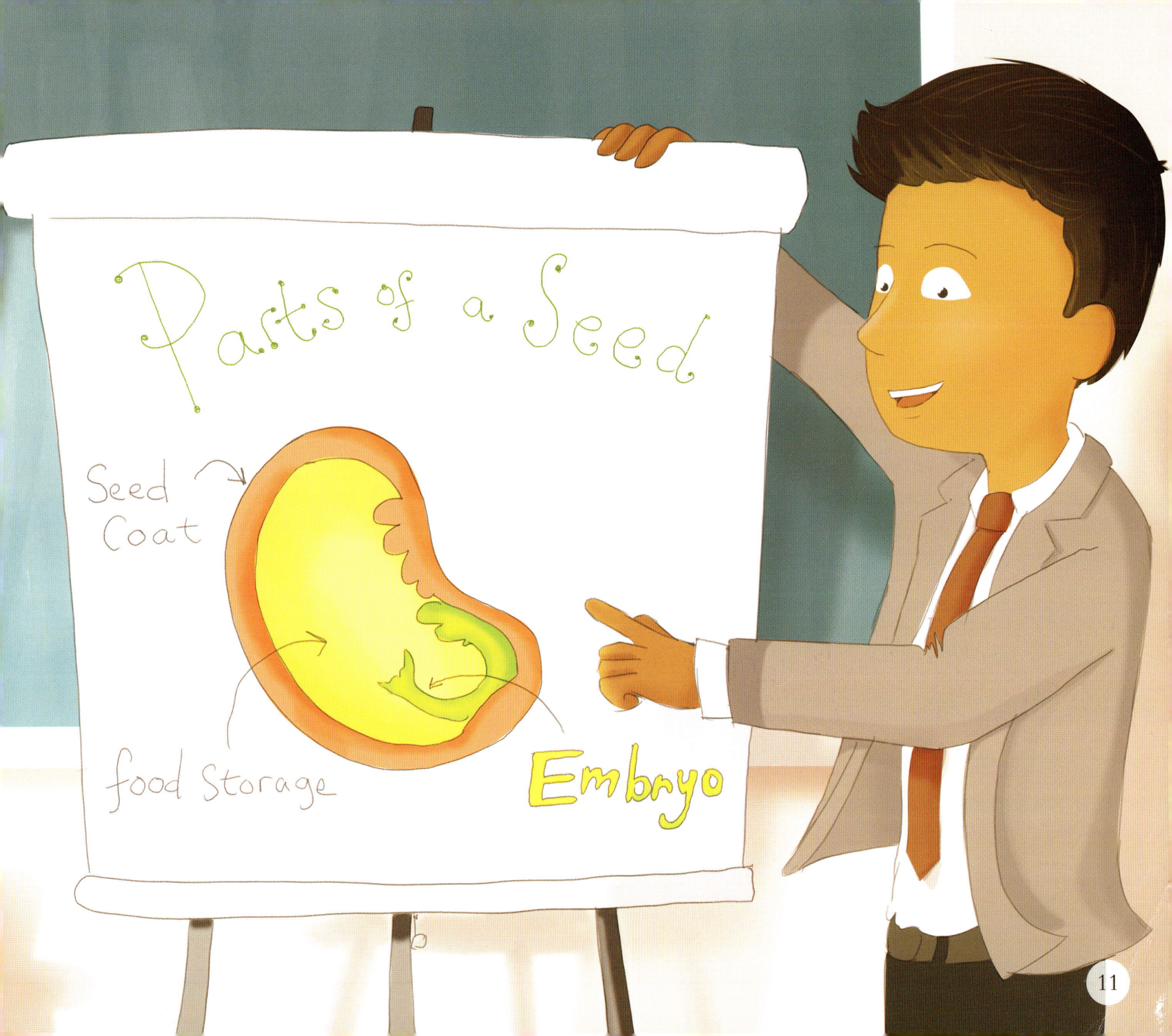
Parts of a Seed
Seed Coat
food Storage
Embryo

Little seeds hold big surprises
of new plants yet to come.

Give seeds warmth. Give them water.
A plant could grow from every one.

13

Curl up like a seed. Close your eyes.
Inside, you hold your big surprise.
You wait and wait so patiently
for spring to bring you what you need.

Ooooooooh, here comes the rain!

Ahhhhhhhh, here comes the sun!

Stretch out your roots. Push up your leaves.

Now you're a **sprout**. Your work is done!

Little seeds hold big surprises
of new plants yet to come.

Give seeds warmth. Give them water.
A plant could grow from every one.

17

Did you know that you can eat seeds: corn and rice and round green peas, lima beans, cocoa beans, coconuts, cashews, almonds, and even peanuts?

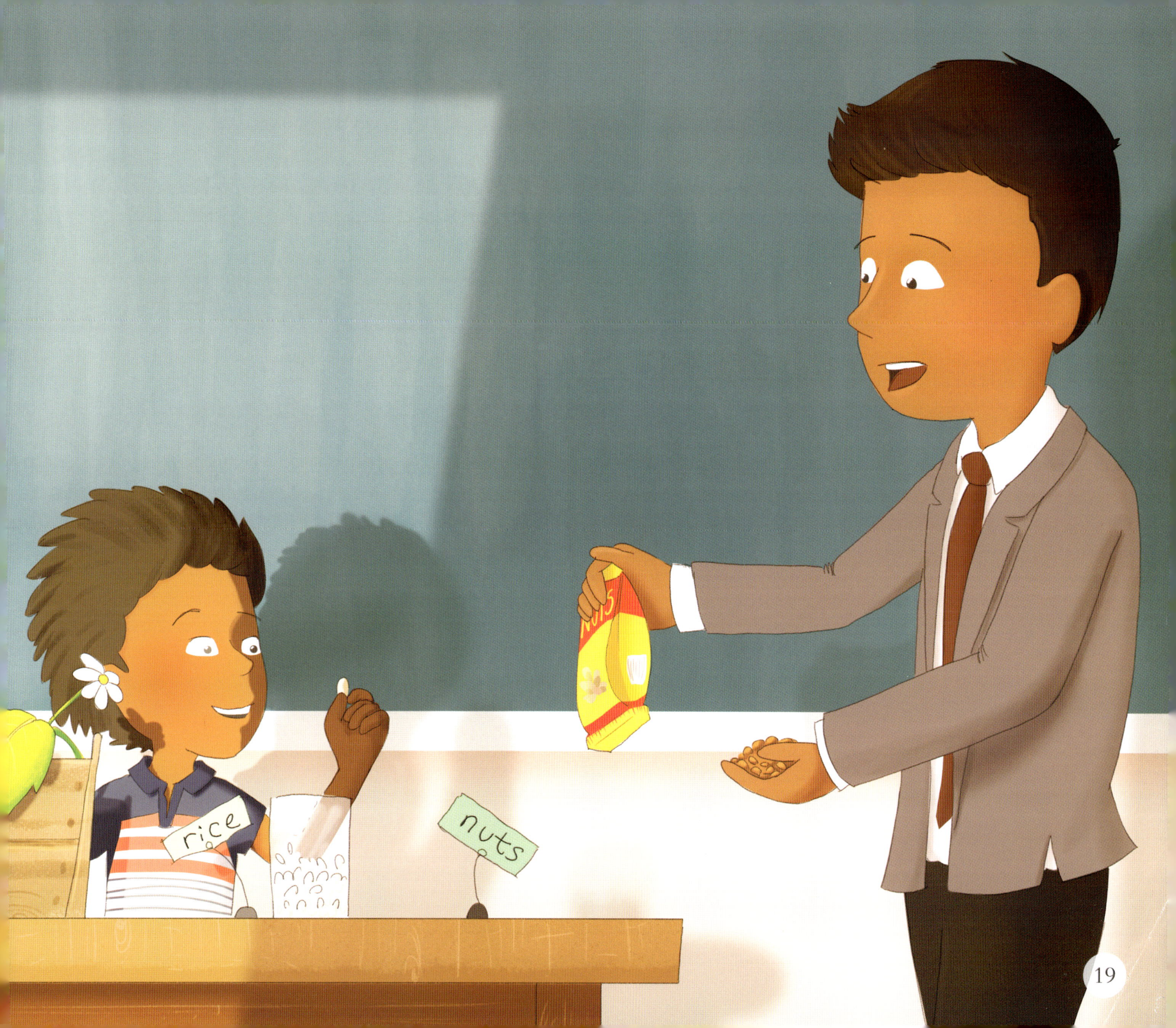
NUTS
rice
nuts

Little seeds hold big surprises
of new plants yet to come.

Give seeds warmth. Give them water.
A plant could grow from every one.

Yeah, a plant could sprout from every one.

SONG LYRICS
Little Seeds

One, two, three, four, five, six!
Six plant parts and they go like this:
roots, stems, leaves,
flowers, fruit, and seeds!

Each part plays a special role.
Seeds help plants grow and grow.

Little seeds hold big surprises
of new plants yet to come.
Give seeds warmth. Give them water.
A plant could grow from every one.

A seed has three parts to help it grow.
A baby plant—that's the embryo.
The rest is food to give it a start.
A tough seed coat forms the outside part.

Little seeds hold big surprises
of new plants yet to come.
Give seeds warmth. Give them water.
A plant could grow from every one.

Curl up like a seed. Close your eyes.
Inside, you hold your big surprise.
You wait and wait so patiently
for spring to bring you what you need.

Ooooooooh, here comes the rain!
Ahhhhhhhh, here comes the sun!
Stretch out your roots. Push up your leaves.
Now you're a sprout. Your work is done!

Little seeds hold big surprises
of new plants yet to come.
Give seeds warmth. Give them water.
A plant could grow from every one.

Did you know that you can eat seeds:
corn and rice and round green peas,
lima beans, cocoa beans, coconuts,
cashews, almonds, and even peanuts?

Little seeds hold big surprises
of new plants yet to come.
Give seeds warmth. Give them water.
A plant could grow from every one.
Yeah, a plant could sprout from every one.

Little Seeds

Hip Hop
Drew Temperante

Intro
One, two, three, four, five, six! Six plant parts and they go like this: roots, stems, leaves, flow-ers, fruit, and seeds! Each part plays a spe-cial role. Seeds help plants grow and grow.

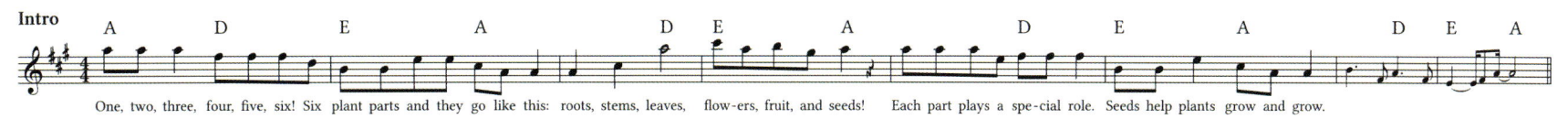

Chorus
Lit-tle seeds hold big sur-pris-es of new plants yet to come. Give seeds warmth. Give them wa-ter. A plant could grow from eve-ry one.

Verse
1. A seed has three parts to help it grow. A ba-by plant— that's the em-bry-o. The rest is food to give it a start. A tough seed coat forms the out-side part.

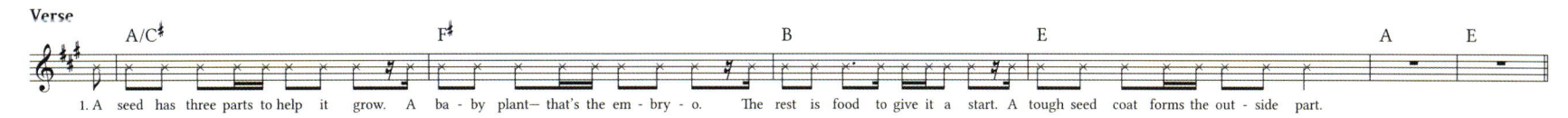

Chorus

Bridge
Curl up like a seed. Close your eyes. In-side, you hold your big sur-prise. You wait and wait so pa-tient-ly for spring to bring you what you need.

Oooooooh, here comes the rain! Ahhhhhhhh, here comes the sun! Stretch out your roots. Push up your leaves. Now you're a sprout. Your work is done!

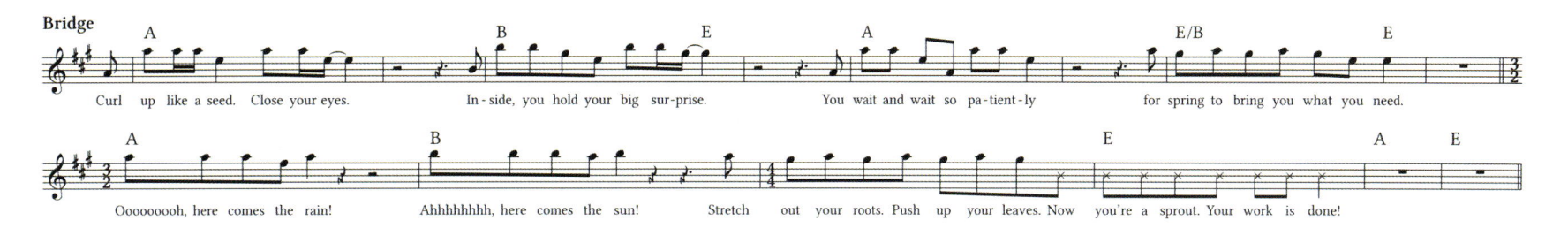

Chorus

Verse 2
Did you know that you can eat seeds:
corn and rice and round green peas,
lima beans, cocoa beans, coconuts,
cashews, almonds, and even peanuts?

Outro
Lit-tle seeds hold big sur-pris-es of new plants yet to come. Give seeds warmth. Give them wa-ter. A plant could grow from eve-ry one. Yeah, a plant could sprout from eve-ry one.

ACCESS THE MUSIC!
SCAN CODE WITH MOBILE APP
CANTATALEARNING.COM

GLOSSARY

coat—a thin outer layer

embryo—a plant in its earliest stage of development

sprout—a new or young plant

GUIDED READING ACTIVITIES

1. This book shows you what seeds look like when they sprout and become plants. Draw a picture of a seed sprouting. Then draw a picture of what the plant will grow up to look like!

2. Put about an inch of water in a glass or jar. Then drop in a few dried beans or grains of brown rice. Watch them for a few days and see if they sprout.

3. Many kinds of seeds are good to eat. What is your favorite? Why?

TO LEARN MORE

Aloian, Molly. *What Are Seeds?* New York: Crabtree, 2012.

Austen, Elizabeth. *Seeds*. Huntington Beach, CA: Teacher Created Materials, 2015.

Bishop, Celeste. *Why Do Plants Have Seeds?* New York: PowerKids Press, 2016.

Throp, Claire. *All about Seeds*. Chicago: Capstone Heinemann Library, 2014.